In Your Face

Adapted by Heather Alexander

Based on the series created by Todd J. Greenwald

Part One is based on the episode, "Pop Me and We Both Go Down," Written by Vince Cheung & Ben Montanio

Part Two is based on the episode, "First Kiss," Written by Vince Cheung & Ben Montanio

New York

PART
ONE

Chapter One

Alex Russo pulled her berry-flavored lip gloss out of her new leather handbag. She swiped it over her lips and then reached for her mini-mirror. She glanced at herself. Perfect! She stretched her arms up over her head and skipped into the Waverly Sub Station, her family's restaurant. Her younger brother, Max, stumbled in behind her, a heavy backpack slung over each shoulder.

"Hey, how was school?" their mom called from behind the counter. "Max!" Theresa Russo gave a little laugh when she spotted her youngest son. "Why are you carrying Alex's backpack like that?"

With the back of his hand, twelve-year-old Max wiped the sweat off his forehead. "She told me my backpack was bending my spine, so she gave me hers to even it out."

"Let's check," Alex said brightly. She slipped her backpack off his right shoulder. She eyed Max critically. "There. All straight. You're welcome."

Her father shot her a disapproving glance. "Alex," Jerry Russo scolded. "Your brother is not your pack mule."

"Yeah, I'm not your pack mule!" Max echoed. It was easier standing up to Alex with his parents around.

"I'm sorry, Maxy," Alex apologized. She handed her backpack to him again. "Could

4

you take this upstairs for me?"

"Sure," Max answered automatically. He headed upstairs to their family's apartment. Max cringed halfway up the stairs. How did Alex do that to him again? Why couldn't he say no to his devious sister?

Sixteen-year-old Justin Russo hurried through the front doors of the restaurant. "Best day at school *ever*!" he cried.

Mrs. Russo looked up from the submarine sandwich she was making. "Oh, they found the guy that was putting peanut butter in your locker?"

"No, but this made me forget about that," Justin replied. "Okay, so I'm in biology, right? Mr. Medina has us pick lab partners, and, like always, my partner ends up being the frog I'm dissecting." Justin hung his head in embarrassment. He didn't run with the popular crowd at school—to put it nicely.

Alex waved her hand. "I have the opposite

problem. Everybody wants me to be their lab partner."

Justin chuckled at his sister. "But you don't take biology."

"That's what I keep telling those guys!" Alex beamed. Popularity was her middle name.

"But then," Justin said, continuing his story, "in walks this brand-new girl, and she is the hottest thing I've ever seen in my life."

Mr. Russo's eyes opened wide, and he leaned over the counter. "Eva Longoria goes to your school?"

"Eva Longoria?" Mrs. Russo suspiciously asked her husband.

Mr. Russo gave an embarrassed laugh and blushed, realizing he'd just stuck his foot in his mouth. "Continue, son," he said, hoping to change the subject.

"So Mr. Medina assigns the beautiful Miranda Hampson to be my lab partner—"

"Miranda Hampson?" Alex interrupted. "Isn't she that new Goth girl in the eleventh grade?"

Justin shook his head. "She's not Goth," he insisted. "She just likes wearing black, and dark makeup, and listens to bands that are kind of scary."

Alex smiled. Her geeky older brother was *so* not clued in. "Oh. *So* not Goth. But Goth," she teased. She perched herself on one of the spinning stools in front of the counter.

"You're missing my point." Justin gritted his teeth. Alex could be such a know-it-all sometimes. "I'm in the tenth grade. She's an older woman."

"Attaboy!" Mr. Russo walked over and slapped Justin on the back. "Like your mother."

Mrs. Russo glared at her husband.

"My story gets better," Justin said, sliding between his parents. "So, me and my Miran— that's my cute nickname for her," Justin

7

cleared his throat dramatically. "—accidentally reached for the scalpel at the same time, and our hands touched, and she didn't pull away. For three seconds." He smiled. "How's that for a great day?"

Alex twirled on her stool. She pointed toward a girl dressed all in black walking through the front door. "Oh, look. Miranda's here. I guess your great day's still going on—*or* coming to a tragic end." She delighted in the look of shock on Justin's face. "Let's watch, boys and girls."

Justin nervously cleared his throat. It was one thing to talk to Miranda in biology class over the comfort of dissecting a frog. It was another to have her here—now—standing in his family's restaurant with Alex and his parents as an audience. "Hey, Miran." He tried to sound upbeat but casual.

Miranda wrinkled her forehead. "Who's Miran?"

"You. Remember?" Justin laughed. Please let her remember, he thought.

"Oh." She tucked a piece of her dark hair dyed with long, white streaks behind her triple-pierced ear.

"I called you that in lab?" Justin reminded her.

Miranda nodded. "Oh, right. I thought you were swallowing and talking at the same time."

"He does generate a lot of saliva," Alex piped up from behind her.

"I have overactive glands," Justin explained. "We're looking into it."

"It was worse when he was a baby," Mr. Russo added with a chuckle. "We had to wrap his head in a diaper."

"Excuse me one second," Justin said to Miranda. He shot his dad a warning glance.

Mr. Russo caught Justin's eye and pretended to be busy refilling the ketchup bottles.

Justin turned back to Miranda. "Do you

need to copy my biology notes or something?"
Justin was used to kids asking for help with
homework.

"No, I—I just came to ask you something."
She smiled. "Are you going to the junior prom?"

"Nah," he replied. "I already told them I
don't want to work lights this year." He didn't
get why the smart kids at school *always* had to
be the tech guys.

Miranda laughed. "You are so funny."

Justin laughed nervously. He hadn't tried to
be funny.

"No, I mean, would you like to go to the
prom with me?" Miranda asked. She took a
deep breath. "I'm—I'm new at school, and I
don't know a lot of guys, and you seem very
nice," she stammered.

"Me?" Justin was momentarily frozen. A
girl had just asked him out? To the prom?
He never thought he could get a girl like
Miranda—not without using magic skills. He

smiled to himself—Miranda was actually cool enough to, maybe, not be freaked out that he came from a family of wizards who could do magic spells. Of course, he knew he couldn't tell her about that. It was a BIG secret. He'd have to continue pretending he was just a normal guy. Suddenly, he jolted awake from his daydream. Normal guys answered girls who asked them out, he realized. "Well, uh, you know, I'll have to check my schedule and—"

"Are you trying to be cool?" Miranda interrupted.

Justin gave Miranda a sheepish grin. "Yeah."

"Don't do that," she teased. "I'm really tired of cool guys," she explained.

Justin laughed. "Good. Because I'm *so* not cool."

He could hear Alex snicker behind him, but he didn't care. He was going to the junior prom with Miranda Hampson! Nothing could beat that.

Chapter Two

"With the *Murrieta-animata* spell, you can make any object come alive," Mr. Russo explained to Alex, Justin, and Max the next afternoon. With a long wooden pointer, he tapped the chalkboard behind him, where the words *Murrieta-animata* were written. The Russo siblings were attending wizard training in the basement of their apartment, which they referred to as "the lair." Their dad taught the lessons every Tuesday and Thursday after school. He had lost all of his wizard powers when he married their mom, a mortal, so he didn't have any actual powers himself. But the Russo kids inherited his family's powers, so Mr. Russo was able to teach them cool spells and tricks.

Alex leaned back on the velvet sofa and gazed around the cluttered room. She'd been down here many times, but each time she was amazed by how totally cool it was. The room was secret. They entered through a door disguised to look like a freezer in the Waverly Sub Station's kitchen. It was a magical room filled with potions, books of spells, and lots of other enchanted things.

The weird thing about being a wizard, Alex realized, was that you weren't born holding a magic wand and the ability to do awesome tricks. It was kind of like learning to ride a bike. You needed someone to teach you what to do. You needed to practice. Magic was often tricky. So many times she'd thought she was doing a certain spell and then—*boom!*—something completely wacky happened.

"Max, you're up," Mr. Russo called. "See what you can do with that cup." He pointed to an orange ceramic mug on the wooden coffee table.

Max squeezed his eyes shut. "*Murrieta-animata,*" he chanted. A moment later, he opened his eyes and stared at the mug in disappointment. It looked exactly the same. A plain old mug. Nothing had happened.

Mr. Russo took a closer look. "Are you picturing it with arms and legs?" he asked, trying to understand what went wrong.

"No," Max said. He pointed to the drawings his father had made on the chalkboard. One was of a block of Swiss cheese, and the next was the same hunk of cheese with a pair of arms and legs. "I'm thinking about cheese."

"No," Mr. Russo sighed. "We don't have any cheese. We have a *cup*. Justin, you're up."

Justin, who was doodling in his notebook, wasn't listening at all.

"Justin! Justin!" their dad called.

Justin's head popped up. "What? What? Oh, uh, sorry, Dad. Um . . ." His face turned bright red.

"You're not paying attention," Mr. Russo accused. "That isn't like you."

"Yeah," Alex agreed. "It's like *me*." Alex had a tendency during wizard class to become easily distracted with other things.

Mr. Russo looked at his son curiously. "What's up, Justin?"

"It's Miranda. It's—it's her junior prom," he admitted. "There's going to be dancing and a lot of time to talk, and I'm kind of nervous."

Mr. Russo threw his arms up in frustration. "Well, *I'm* kind of nervous—no one is paying attention to the lesson!" he cried.

"I am," Alex piped up. "It's easy."

Justin rolled his eyes. His sister never took

15

notes at school and barely listened during wizard lessons.

Their dad smiled. "All right," he told Alex. "Put your magic where your mouth is."

Alex sighed. When would her family realize that she paid attention when it was important? At least, she did sometimes. She glanced around the room. The orange cup looked so boring. Her gaze landed on the gold trophy next to it. A shiny little metal man stood on a pedestal, as if he were frozen in place while sprinting. Suddenly, she had an idea. She pointed to the trophy. "'*Murrieta-animata*,'" she announced.

Her dad watched the cup intently. It still looked the same. "Alex, what did you just do?" he asked.

"I did the spell you wanted. You're welcome." She sighed. Where were the congratulations? She thought she was pretty good at this wizard stuff.

Suddenly, the trophy-man leaped up.

"Hello, losers! See you at the finish line!" he shouted. Then he jumped off his pedestal. Landing on a wooden table, he raced across it and then hopped off the edge onto the carpet. In a flash, he was gone!

Mr. Russo looked at Alex in frustration. "We're supposed to be doing the spell on the cup!" he exclaimed.

"Well, the trophy seemed easier—it already has legs," she explained.

Alex heard her father groan. Uh-oh! He was upset. "Sorry, Dad," she said meekly.

Mr. Russo shook his head sternly. "Sorry, nothing. That was the 'First Place in State' trophy I got in high school. You better find that, young lady, before your mom sees it. You know how she hates magic running amok."

"Plus, she's still mad about all that stuff you said about Eva Longoria," Max pointed out to his dad.

Alex knew a good distraction when she

heard one. "Yeah, Mom was pretty upset about all that. Let's relive it," she suggested, hoping to turn her dad's attention away from the missing trophy-man. "We'll play parts. I call Mom."

"Stop trying to change the subject," her dad said in annoyance. After all these years, he knew her tricks. "The rest of the lesson was going to be about how we un-animate stuff we've animated, and now we can't do that until you find the trophy." Mr. Russo tossed his wooden pointer on the floor. "Class is over."

"Great," Justin grumbled, standing up. "I'm already nervous about Miranda, and now I've got to worry about finding this stupid trophy."

Alex patted her brother on the back. "Sounds like you've got a lot on your plate. Let me know how that all works out for you." She headed up the stairs toward the kitchen. If Justin was going to look for the trophy-man, maybe she could make a pit stop at the freezer for a little ice cream!

The next day, Alex and Max sat in the kitchen, watching their parents make breakfast. They loved watching their parents cook together. Her mom danced and sang as she added spice after spice to whatever was on the stove. Alex's dad always complained that Mrs. Russo's singing made concentrating on the recipes impossible. But Mrs. Russo just laughed. She didn't believe in recipes. She said you had to *feel* it when you cooked.

"Guys, which is better for prom?" Justin asked, holding up two jackets in front of him as he walked into the kitchen.

Alex leaped off her stool. Fashion was her thing. She inspected the choices. "Well, the tux says, 'Safe boy.' But the zebra jacket says, 'Danger, danger, stay away from my daughter.' Goth girl will like you for that."

Justin lowered his arms to get a better look at the two jackets.

"Whoa!" Max cried, as Justin's face came into view.

"Nice one!" Mr. Russo chuckled.

"Ew!" Alex clapped her hand over her mouth in horror.

Justin couldn't believe how they were reacting to the jackets. They weren't *that* bad. "You guys can never agree on anything."

"Yeah, but I think we pretty much agree *that's* the biggest zit we've ever seen." Alex pointed to Justin's forehead.

"What zit?' he asked.

Max reached for the big silver serving spoon his father was holding and handed it to Justin to use as a mirror. Justin's eyes grew wide as he stared at his reflection. "Oh, uh, well, it can't be that big, can it? Maybe . . . maybe the mirror is like a carnival mirror." He quickly turned the spoon and gazed into its flip side. Please, oh, please, show me something different, he pleaded silently.

No. There it was. A huge, bright red pimple. Justin screamed. It was horrendous!

His father tried to make him feel better. "You can hardly see it."

But Justin wasn't buying it. It was the biggest zit he had ever seen in his life!

His mother hurried over to him. "My baby has a zit *como una montaña*!" She turned to Alex, who wasn't the best at understanding Spanish. "That means 'like a mountain.'"

Justin groaned. "This is going to ruin everything. I can't take Miranda to the prom looking like this."

"Why not?" Alex joked. "She *does* like danger. If you go with that thing, she'll never know when it's going to blow."

Justin raced up the spiral staircase to the bathroom. He scrutinized his face in the mirror. The angle or the amount of light shining on it didn't matter. It was horrible. How would he ever face Miranda?

He trudged back to the kitchen. Mrs. Russo was stirring something in a huge pot on the stove. He flopped onto a stool by the counter and dropped his head into his hands. "What was I thinking getting involved with an older woman?"

Mrs. Russo hurried over and wrapped her arms around him. "*Papito*, calm down. I've got an old Mexican remedy here that is much safer than popping it. My grandmother created it. It works every time."

Justin raised his head and gazed at the steaming pot. There was hope! "Thanks, Mom."

His mom scooped a bowl full of a grayish paste out of the pot. With a wooden spoon, she gently patted the paste across his forehead. Justin wrinkled his nose at the sour smell. "We just smear a little bit of this on," his mom explained, "then we wrap it tight in a banana bandanna." She wound a huge green banana leaf around his head. "And in three days, gone."

Justin bolted upright. "Three days? The prom is tomorrow, Mom."

Mrs. Russo bit her lip, thinking hard. "I just remembered a quicker remedy." She grabbed him by the arm and led him up the stairs, toward the bathroom. "Okay, I'm going to need rubbing alcohol, a wire brush, and a towel for you to bite on."

"What? No!" Justin shrieked. Even getting his finger pricked at the doctor made him squeamish. There was no way his mother was attacking his pimple with a wire brush!

There has to be another way, he thought. There just has to!

Chapter Three

Later that day, Alex, holding a metal detector, slowly walked up the stairs in their apartment. One . . . *beep!* . . . two . . . *beep!* . . . three . . . She stopped and glanced around. She didn't get it. The trophy-man had to be close, because the detector kept beeping. But she couldn't find it anywhere! She'd been up and down these stairs, like, fifty times already! She sighed in frustration.

She headed back down the stairs again. She

waved the long metal detector pole back and forth. *Beep! Beep!*

She groaned loudly. "This thing keeps beeping," she told Justin, who was watching her from the family-room sofa. "The metal man must be close."

Justin rolled his eyes. "Alex, you're on a metal staircase with a *metal* detector."

"Oh, I just wasted an hour going up and down these things," she huffed. She skipped down the rest of the stairs and tossed the metal detector in a corner. She stopped short, noticing her brother's forehead. "Ugh!" she cried. "That puppy's ginormous!"

Justin cringed. He had just finished convincing himself it wasn't so bad. But obviously he was wrong.

"Why don't we just use the acne spell I use to keep my skin clear and velvety smooth?" Alex suggested. She ran her hand across one of her unblemished cheeks.

"Alex, you're chasing a metal man," Justin pointed out. "I don't think magic's your thing."

She grabbed Justin's chin and studied his face. "I'm doing you a favor," she explained. "Just hold your head still, okay?"

Justin squirmed, "Alex, don't!"

"*Jolovitz-rid-of-zitz*—" she began to chant. Justin lurched backward, freeing his face from her grasp. "Please, I'm working," she insisted. Alex reached for him again. "*Jolovitz-rid-of . . . Murrieta-animata . . .*"

"Magic only causes trouble," Justin interrupted, still squirming.

Alex suddenly leaped backward.

"What?' Justin cried. "Is it gone? Did it work?"

"Not exactly," said a man's voice.

Alex gasped and stared in disbelief at Justin's forehead. "Your zit just talked to me!" she exclaimed.

"You should hear me sing. *Me-me-me-me-me-me-me!* I'll do anything but country," the voice from the zit said.

Alex peered at the pimple in fascination. There was actually a tiny man's face with a beard and beady eyes in the middle of Justin's zit. And it could talk!

"What did you just do?" Justin demanded.

"I—I don't know," Alex stammered. "You were yelling at me. I got confused. It's all your fault. Dad said to never yell at someone when they're doing a spell."

Alex stared at the blemish on her brother's forehead. "He's already mad about the trophy. If he finds out about this, we're both hosed."

"Excuse me, *you're* hosed," Justin corrected her. "*You* did this. I'm just the guy with a big, gross, talking zit on my forehead!"

"*Hel-lo*?" called the zit. "I'm right here."

"Alex, get this thing off me!" Justin screamed.

At that moment, Max rushed down the

stairs and over to the sofa. His hands were cupped together in front of him. "I caught the trophy-man!" Max exclaimed, triumphant. "It was easy. He was on the hamster wheel. The hamster—not too happy about it."

"See, Justin?" Alex said, perking up. "Now Dad will teach us the un-animation spell, and your zit problem will be over."

"Boy, I didn't even get a chance to spend Christmas with you guys," the zit joked.

Max's eyes lit up as he studied his brother's forehead. "You animated Justin's zit? Sweet. I want one."

"Oh, no, you don't," Justin warned.

Max flinched and raised his hands. "Ow! Trophy-man kicked me."

The tiny metal man burst through Max's fists, jogging in place on his wrist. "Keep on trucking!" he sang out before dashing up Max's sleeve.

Max began to wiggle and squirm. "Whoa! Hey! He's in my shirt!"

Alex and Justin could see a lump under the fabric racing up and down Max's arm.

"It tickles!" Max cried, as the trophy-man ran around his leg. Max flopped onto the sofa in a fit of giggles. The trophy-man suddenly stopped tickling Max and ran away.

Meanwhile, Justin had found a mirror. He stared wide-eyed at the scruffy man's face popping out of the enormous growth on his forehead. "That's it. I'm calling Miranda and telling her I can't take her to the prom."

"No, no, no. Wait." Alex hurried over to him. She felt really bad. "I—I can talk to Dad. I'm not going to let my brother miss out on what might be his only prom because of some ugly, hideous thing on his face."

"You guys are really rude to company," the zit complained.

Justin clapped his hand over his head to shut it up. Alex was usually an expert at sweet-talking their dad to get what she wanted.

She'll do it, he told himself. He couldn't bear to think what would happen if she couldn't get the spell—and he was forced to live with a living, breathing, *talking* zit.

Chapter Four

Alex watched as her father eased out a tray of freshly baked rolls from the huge oven in the Waverly Sub Station's kitchen. She inhaled the homemade aroma. "Mmm ... Daddy, your bread's so good, it's—it's *inspirational*."

Mr. Russo beamed proudly. A New York City magazine had recently called his sub rolls some of the best in Manhattan.

"In fact, it makes me want to be a better

person," Alex continued. "And I think I'm going to start with wizards' training."

Mr. Russo placed the tray on the counter and looked at his daughter quizzically. *"Really?"*

"Hey, here's an awesome idea I just thought of right now." Alex bounced on her toes, hoping her enthusiasm was contagious. "Why don't you give me the un-animation spell you were going to teach us, and I'll start working on it?"

Her dad chuckled. "Oh, yeah. Why don't I just give you the whole spell book—we'll just call you a wizard," he replied sarcastically.

Alex wrinkled her nose. "That sounds like a lot of reading. I'll just take the one spell for now."

Her dad shook his head. "Look, with wizardry comes responsibility, and that also means taking care of your mistakes. I'm not giving you that spell until you find that trophy."

Alex considered pleading. Begging. Even shedding a few tears. But one look at her dad's face and she knew he meant business. No trophy, no spell. And with no spell, Alex was sure her dad would discover she made Justin's zit come to life. That would get her in even more trouble!

She headed out of the kitchen, determined to find the missing man from the trophy. "Where are you, trophy-man?" she called. "Mom has a bowling trophy, and she's really cute." She hoped that would bring him out of hiding. Alex headed up the back staircase that led to their apartment. Justin was waiting for her by the door.

"Please tell me you got the un-animation spell from Dad," he said with anticipation.

"I got the un-animation spell from Dad," Alex fibbed.

Justin's eyes lit up. "Oh, really?"

"No," Alex admitted. "I just felt like I owed you some good news."

Justin could feel the disappointment in the pit of his stomach.

His sister stood on tiptoe and peered at his face. "Yikes, that thing is so big I can't stop looking at it. But don't worry. I have a better plan. We're going to pop the stupid thing."

"Wait!" yelled the zit. "I can help you with the girl."

"What?" Justin asked. He was still having trouble believing that a pimple on his face could talk.

"Don't listen to him," Alex cautioned.

"Justin, I can really help you!" the zit exclaimed.

Justin was intrigued. "How?'

"You were great with the girl in biology, right?" the zit asked. "What were you like outside of class?"

"I don't know," Justin replied uncertainly.

"I don't know," the zit cruelly mimicked.

"Hold on," Alex said, stepping closer to the zit. "What could you do for him?"

"Talk him through the rough spots," the zit

explained. He smiled at Alex. "He is going with a girl almost as pretty as you."

Alex grinned at the compliment. "Oh, he's good," she told Justin. "But I think it's a mistake," she added.

"I know what they want to hear," the zit said convincingly. "I know what you should say to them. Give me a chance," the zit pleaded. "Come on."

"Maybe I *could* use a wing-zit," Justin mused. Desperate times definitely called for desperate actions, he thought. And, boy, am I desperate!

Alex stared at him in disbelief. "Yep. I see nothing wrong with letting a growth on your face tell you what to say to a girl." She sighed. "Good luck."

But she knew Justin needed more than luck.

She hurried to the kitchen and threw open the cabinets. She needed to find that little metal trophy-dude, fast!

Chapter Five

Justin wished he could stop his heart from beating so loudly. He was sure all the other kids could hear it above the pounding beat of the hip-hop music in the hotel ballroom. He never thought the prom would be so scary. Then again, he'd never thought he'd actually *be* at the dance in the first place.

Justin and Miranda had just arrived at the dance a few minutes earlier, and so far, so good.

Miranda was saying hi to a friend so Justin had a few moments alone to take a deep breath and renew his composure. He stood in front of the refreshment table and adjusted his black fedora. He had to give Alex credit. She'd paired the zebra-print jacket with a cool hat, so now he not only looked good but, more importantly, the gigantic zit was hidden from Miranda and everyone else.

"You're going to have to stop sweating. It's getting into my eyes," the zit grumbled from under the hat.

Justin whirled around. Did anyone hear that? he wondered. Everyone seemed to be paired off or in groups, dancing and talking. No one seemed to have spotted anything. And Miranda was too busy comparing dresses with some girls in the corner to have noticed.

"When are you going to start helping me?" Justin whispered to his zit man. "I've been talking about biology. That's all I've got."

"I know," the zit sneered. "She almost jumped out of the cab when you kept going on and on about deoxyribonucleic acid. Just say what I say."

"Here she comes," Justin whispered. He watched nervously as Miranda approached. She walked with such confidence. She didn't seem to care what anyone thought or said. He wished he could be like that.

"Well, Denise says we look cute together," Miranda reported. "And she loves your jacket." She gave him an encouraging smile.

Justin felt his palms beginning to sweat. Miranda looked so pretty in her red-and-black dress. Now what do I do? he wondered.

Suddenly he heard a voice whisper from under his hat. "You're the one who looks great."

"Thank you," Justin whispered back.

The zit sighed in frustration. "Not you," he whispered, "the girl."

"Oh," Justin whispered. He focused on

Miranda and cleared his throat. "You're the one who looks great," he told her.

Her cheeks turned slightly pink. "Well, thanks. You're sweet." She giggled.

"No, you're sweet," Justin replied, without hesitation.

"That's lame," his zit scolded him in a whisper. "Don't ad lib."

"Right," Justin said under his breath. He could feel an awkward silence settle between him and Miranda.

"Well, you want to dance?" she asked finally.

"Sure." He followed her out to the crowded dance floor. "What do you know about dancing?" he quietly asked the zit.

"Nothing, I'm a zit," it hissed. "Put the hat down. I don't want to see this train wreck."

Justin had been secretly watching the other kids on the dance floor and tried to mimic some of their moves. He yanked his fedora over one eye and began flailing his arms and tried to pop his hips.

Miranda gave a little laugh as a crowd gathered around him. She liked his energy and enthusiasm. "You're a really good dancer."

"Justin's got a girlfriend," the zit whispered in a singsong voice.

"She's not my girlfriend," he insisted. But at that very moment, the pounding song ended, and the DJ transitioned into a quiet ballad. Suddenly, Justin's voice sounded much louder than he'd intended.

"Girlfriend?" Miranda asked curiously. She stopped dancing and stared at him.

Justin froze.

"Oops, don't panic," advised the zit. "Hang in there."

Justin gave Miranda a tentative nod. He wasn't sure what else to do. He certainly didn't trust himself to speak.

"What? Okay. I'm your girlfriend," Miranda said with a smile. She reached for his hand and led him back toward the refreshment table.

Justin smiled and gave a little chuckle. "Wow, I never thought I'd be so grateful to a zit," he whispered. He poured two cups of soda for them.

"Now you got your girl. Now it's time for the Z-Man to have some fun," the zit announced. His small eyes widened when he spotted a cute girl standing next to Justin. "Hey!" the zit cried, this time loud enough for everyone around to hear. "You come with a fire extinguisher? Because you're smoking hot!"

"What?" Miranda stepped closer to Justin. "How did you do that?'

"Uh . . ." Justin found himself laughing nervously as he searched his brain for an explanation. "Do what?"

"I thought I heard you talking while you were drinking," Miranda said. She seemed confused.

Justin waved his hand as if what she'd just

said was ridiculous. "That wasn't me." He quickly took a sip of soda. He had to do something about this situation—and fast.

"Uh, hold on," he told Miranda. He stepped to the side, out of her earshot. "What are you doing?" he demanded in a hushed whisper to the pimple.

"Oh, come on, dude. Lighten up," the zit scolded. "I got you the girl. Now it's *my* turn to have some fun."

At that moment, a pretty girl in a red dress walked by. "Hey, beautiful!" the zit shouted. Justin cringed. He knew the girl thought *he* was taunting her. "Can I talk to your boyfriend?" the zit continued. Then he made horrible chimp sounds, as if her boyfriend was a monkey. The girl clasped her hand over her mouth and ran out into the hallway. Justin hoped she wasn't going to find her boyfriend. She was dating a guy on the wrestling team!

"That's it. I'm popping you," Justin told the zit. He couldn't figure out any other way to shut up his out-of-control pimple!

"Not so fast, lover boy," the zit warned. "Get a load of me. I'm engorged. You pop me and we both go down." The zit gave an evil, maniacal laugh.

"Hey, zebra!" the girl's boyfriend called from across the dance floor. He was flanked by two of his huge wrestling buddies. "Were you making monkey sounds at me?"

Justin's eyes widened, and he could feel his lungs tighten, making it hard to breathe. This was trouble. I'll just apologize, he decided, and hopefully he'll let me go.

But before he could speak, the zit's voice rang out loud and clear: "Oh, look who learned his animals!"

The large wrestler stared at Justin in disbelief.

Justin groaned. He was toast.

Chapter Six

Back at the Russo's apartment, Max wandered into the living room, where Alex was hanging out on the couch.

"Hey, you caught the trophy-man!" Max exclaimed. He hurried over to Alex on the sofa.

She stared proudly at the little metal man, trapped on the coffee table in front of her. "Nothing like a duct-tape finish line to save the day," she said with a smirk as the trophy man squirmed, trying to free himself from the sticky, thick silver tape. She had written the word FINISH across the tape and hung it over the table, and the little dude had fallen for it.

Suddenly, Alex's phone trilled the opening notes of her favorite song. She pulled the slim pink phone out of her pocket and checked the caller ID. "Oh, it's Justin," she told Max. She flipped it open. "Hey! How's prom? *What*?" she asked in disbelief. "Huge eleventh graders?"

Max raised his eyebrows. This didn't sound good.

"How many?" Alex asked. Her face was serious, her forehead wrinkled in thought. "Look, I feel bad. I'll get the spell from Dad, and I'll be there as fast as I can." She put down her phone and stood up.

"Max, I got to go help Justin at prom. Go get my jacket, the really cute one. The one that cinches at the waist with the buttons. Go!" she commanded. "Oh! And my matching purse!" she added.

"I know the one!" Max called, taking the steps to their bedrooms two at a time.

At that moment, Mr. Russo walked through the front door. He had worked long after the restaurant had closed—cleaning things up, organizing, and working on new sandwich recipes.

"Daddy!" Alex cried, hurrying over to him. "I caught the trophy-man."

He gave Alex a huge grin. "Great!"

"You want to give me the un-animation spell now?" Alex asked. She hoped she didn't sound too desperate. She really didn't want to have to explain the talking zit on her brother's forehead to her dad!

"Look, before we get into that, we need to sit down and have a long, serious talk." Mr. Russo made himself comfortable on the sofa, leaning back against the cushions.

Alex knew what this meant. Her dad was preparing for one of his famous, rambling lectures that lasted *forever*. She had to move things along—and fast. "I know. I know. I'm grounded for three weeks."

Her dad looked surprised. "How did you come up with three weeks?"

"One for using magic behind your back, another for letting the trophy-man run around the house, and the last one for future trouble I'll probably be getting in." Alex smiled at her dad. Hopefully, this will work, she thought.

Her dad stared at her curiously. Then he shrugged. "Well, that's one more week than I would have come up with, but we'll go with that." He patted the sofa beside him, and Alex sat down. "Okay, say '*Garibay-immobilitay*.'"

Alex pointed to the struggling trophy-man. "*Garibay-immobilitay*." Suddenly the trophy-man froze!

"Great!" Mr. Russo beamed. "Even though I don't got it anymore, I still got it. I like the way I deal with problems." He leaned back,

47

proud of how everything had turned out.

Max raced down the stairs. He handed Alex her jacket. Then he held up a hip leather bag. "I think this purse goes better with this jacket."

Alex nodded her approval.

Mr. Russo stared in disbelief. Was his youngest son really giving his daughter fashion advice? "Now I've got another problem," he moaned.

Meanwhile, back at the prom, Justin found himself surrounded by three of the biggest eleventh graders he'd ever seen. Justin knew he had no chance when it came to fighting. His only hope—and it was slim at best—was to talk his way out of this mess. "Guys, when I implied you didn't know your animals, what I really meant was . . ." Actually, he wasn't sure what he meant. He tried a different approach. "You know, three against one isn't fair!"

The girl's boyfriend sneered. "I don't know

a lot of what you just said, but let's see if you can say it again without any teeth." He grabbed Justin by the collar of his jacket, pulling him close. Justin winced.

"Hey, Brian!" Miranda suddenly called out. He loosened his grip on Justin's jacket and whirled around. "There's some loser in the hallway who says you can't do twenty finger-tip push-ups."

Brian dropped Justin and flexed his muscles. "Everyone knows I can do fifty," he announced loudly. "Come on," he called to his two friends standing next to him. "Let's go show them." They hurried toward the hallway, with a crowd of kids following enthusiastically.

Justin sighed. That was way too close, he thought. "Thanks, Miranda." He gave her a grateful smile.

But she didn't smile back. She stood with her hands on her hips. "Don't thank me. I just want to know what's going on. You're acting like two different people."

"Yeah, I'm sorry." Do I dare tell her the truth? he debated with himself. No way. Even a girl as cool as Miranda can't handle a talking zit! "I know I'm being weird. It's just that I really like you, and nothing's going right." This is true, Justin thought.

Miranda nodded. "I like you, too," she said softly.

"Can we start all over?" Justin asked.

"Sure." Miranda reached her arms around his neck and hugged him.

"Just a hug?" cracked the zit, loud enough for Miranda to hear. "I can get that from Grandma. How about some lip action?"

Miranda shoved Justin away, startled. "There you go again!" she cried, her eyes blazing. "You're a pig." She turned and hurried toward the door.

"Miranda! Wait!" Justin cried. But she

didn't stop. He was about to go after her, when someone tapped his shoulder.

"Dude, help me out here." It was the DJ, a tall, skinny guy with an enormous Afro. "I need a break. My hair's gone a little flat. I got to go pump it up."

"What?" Justin wasn't sure he'd heard right. This guy wanted *him* to take over? "But—but I'm not—I—" Justin tried to think of an excuse, but all he could focus on was Miranda.

The DJ grabbed Justin by his zebra-print jacket and pulled him behind all the sound equipment. "Don't worry about it," the DJ said. Then he grabbed the microphone and announced, "Yo, everybody listen up. We got a guest DJ in the Kansas Room in the Town and Country Suites." He glanced at Justin, his eyes settling on the black fedora. "Give it up for DJ Mad Hatter!"

Only one or two kids clapped. The rest groaned.

Justin twirled the microphone between his hands. The silence was deafening. He laughed nervously, aware that tons of kids were watching. "Um, Justin in the hiz-house. Let's raise the ceiling. Hoot-hoot." He tried his best DJ impersonation. He could tell by the blank stares that no one was very impressed.

He reached down and flicked a switch. The rhythms of drums and bass guitar filled the room. Kids started dancing again.

"This is a fast one for all the ladies," the zit's voice suddenly announced into the microphone, "because I loves to watch you shake that junk!"

Justin cringed. Can it get any worse than having a rude, nasty-talking zit on my face? he wondered. He didn't think so.

A minute later, he realized he was wrong. It *could* get worse. Brian and his beefy buddies were back.

"There's nobody in the hallway. We must have scared him away!" Brian bellowed. Then he spotted Justin flipping through CDs. "Oh, hey, look! Justin Timber*lame* is up on the DJ stand." He turned to his buddies, an evil grin spreading across his face. "Let's take that freak down."

Justin stared, wide-eyed, as they approached. Miranda wasn't going to save him now. He quickly searched the room for an emergency exit.

"Hey, guys!" called a familiar voice. "You want to dance?"

Justin heaved a sigh of relief as Alex grabbed Brian's arm, stopping him in his tracks.

Brian glanced at Alex. "Why would we want to dance with an eighth grader? Get lost." He shrugged Alex off.

"I'm in *ninth* grade, you big idiots," Alex replied.

Brian paused to think this over. While he stood silently, Alex hurried past him and ran up to Justin. She couldn't wait to try out the spell.

"What took you so long?" Justin demanded. He was still shaking from yet *another* close call.

"Okay, if you really want to know. I missed the A train, so I had to catch the bus on Fourth Street, where a guy was selling the cutest earrings—"

Justin sighed. Alex could babble about fashion for hours, if allowed. "Just do the spell!" he pleaded, pulling off his hat.

"No! Stop! Don't do it!" cried the zit. "I can teach you how to drive!"

Alex pointed at the zit. "*Garibay-immobilitay*," she chanted.

"Oh!" squealed the zit. Suddenly the face on the pimple disappeared!

"Did it work?" Justin asked.

"Yep. You're back to your regular, pimple-faced, dorky self," Alex reported.

"Thanks." Justin smiled at his sister gratefully.

"No, I'm sorry I got you into this," Alex said. "Now go out there and get your older woman."

Justin picked up the microphone and then took a deep breath. "Excuse me," he announced as the song ended. "I'd like to apologize to Miranda Hampson for the way I acted. Miranda?"

A crowd of kids on the dance floor spotted Justin's zit and pointed. "Ew!" they screeched, pointing and laughing.

Justin blushed. He turned to Alex and whispered, "I'm not wearing my hat, am I?"

Alex shook her head. "Pop that sucker and run," she advised. "That's all you've got. See you at home."

Justin took one last look at the grossed-out faces of his classmates and then raced for the door. For him, the prom was officially *over*.

Chapter Seven

Justin sat on a stool in the dark in his family's restaurant. It had been closed for hours, but he didn't mind. He couldn't bear going upstairs and telling his parents how everyone had laughed at his zit, and how he'd ruined everything with Miranda.

He spun around on the stool, deep in thought. Come to think of it, he didn't much care about the kids at school. He knew they'd forget all about him by Monday. Hey, they'd probably forgotten already. It was Miranda that bothered him. He really liked her. And he'd blown it. He knew he could never explain the talking zit, but at the very least, he should have gone after her and tried to come up with some kind of excuse.

"Hey, Justin," a voice said, suddenly interruping Justin's thoughts.

He looked up to see Miranda, who had just entered the restaurant. He stood up nervously. "Oh. Hey, Miranda."

Alex followed behind her. "Miranda wanted to talk to you, because I told her why you were acting so weird."

"Yeah," said Miranda, walking over to him. "Why didn't you just tell me you had a zit? I would've understood. I've got one, too." She pushed her dark bangs aside and smiled shyly.

"Oh, man." Justin tried not to grimace when he saw Miranda's pimple. It was almost as large as his was!

"Yeah, that's a honker," Alex said, leaning over to inspect it.

Miranda and Justin both raised their eyebrows at her.

"Sorry, you two want to be alone." Alex backed up a few feet.

Justin walked Miranda over to a small table and they both sat down. He had to tell her how he felt. It was now or never. "Look, I was so nervous about tonight."

"Why?" Miranda asked.

"Well, because I've never been to a junior prom with an older woman that I really like," Justin blurted out.

"Oh, that's okay," Miranda smiled. "Because I kind of like this one younger guy right now."

Justin's face fell. He'd been right. He *had* blown it. And now she had found some other guy. "Oh, that's cool." He tried his best to hide his disappointment. "I understand. Good luck with him."

Alex literally leaped across the restaurant. How could her brother be so clueless! Didn't he know that Miranda liked him? "She means you!" she shouted.

Justin blushed. "Oh. Right. Yeah, me," he said. He nervously reached out and shook Miranda's hand.

"Well, um, I got to get home," Miraanda said. She smiled and headed toward the door. "See you in school." He watched as she walked out the door.

"Thank you so much for bringing Miranda," he said, turning to Alex.

"That's okay. I kind of owed it to you. You know, giving you the talking zit and everything. But I'm kind of going to miss him. He was the only one around here who was almost as clever as me." Alex grinned smugly.

Justin rolled his eyes. "Yep, you're *so* clever." He opened the door. "Hey, you want to go get some ice cream?"

"Sure," Alex agreed, stepping outside.

Justin closed the door behind her and turned the lock. "Yeah, you're *so* clever," he told his sister through the glass window. "Now you're locked out."

Alex didn't miss a beat. "That's okay. I'll catch up with Miranda and tell her about your doll collection!"

"They're action figures!" he protested.

But as Alex took a few steps down the street, he quickly unlocked the door and opened it wide. He was no fool. He may have gotten away with the talking zit, but he still didn't know enough magic to make a girl—any girl, even Miranda—understand the seriousness of collecting action figures!

PART
TWO

Chapter One

Max Russo leaned into his sandwich and sniffed. *Mmmm!* It smelled delicious. He knew that this creation was like no other he'd made before. And Max had made a lot of sandwiches for a twelve-year-old!

"Now, *this* is why it's great we own a sandwich shop," Max said proudly. He pointed out his latest masterpiece to his older brother, Justin. Max's eyes widened at all of the delicious ingredients he had piled onto the long hoagie roll. He loved that his family owned the Waverly Sub Station, a cool sandwich shop in Greenwich Village. It was a unique blue-and-white tiled restaurant that was designed to look like just like a real New York City subway station. He was getting really good at creating new sandwiches to bring to school for lunch every day. It sure beat having to eat that stuff the cafeteria called food!

Justin glanced up from the sandwich he was making for his own lunch. He gasped in disbelief. "Are those *mashed potatoes* on a sand-wich?"

Max nodded. "On a bed of chicken strips with a peanut butter blanket." He placed the top of the roll on his sandwich. "What did you make?" he asked Justin.

"A sandwich, not a Dumpster," Justin replied. He held up his normal-looking sandwich tucked into a plastic baggie. "Tuna fish on wheat."

Max sighed. His sixteen-year-old brother was

supersmart—and super*boring*! Justin had no imagination. It was amazing they were related.

Harper Evans leaned over the tiled counter and gasped. "Tuna fish on *wheat*?" she squealed. "That's going to be *our* sandwich."

Fourteen-year-old Harper smiled, a faraway look in her eyes. She had a huge crush on Justin. But he didn't realize that they were destined to be together. But that didn't matter to Harper. She knew he'd come around. Someday.

"Do you know what our song is?" she asked with a nervous giggle. Being around Justin always made her do that.

Justin shrugged. Harper was nice enough as his sister Alex's best friend, but it kind of creeped him out the way she was always staring at him. He spotted Miranda entering the restaurant. "Hey, there's my girlfriend!"

Harper's eyes lit up. "That sounds like a cute song." Maybe Justin really does like me! she thought.

Suddenly, she spotted Justin talking to Miranda Hampson. Her heart sank. He hadn't meant *Harper* was his girlfriend.

Meanwhile, Max started to wrap up his sandwich. He hoped he had enough time to race upstairs to their apartment above the restaurant and sneak in a few games on the computer before school.

"That's a nice-looking sandwich," a voice suddenly said. Max looked up to see a man in a suit and tie standing in front of the counter. "What do you call it?" the man asked.

Max glanced back down at his sandwich. " 'To the Max!' " he blurted out, with a huge grin on his face.

The man nodded. "I'll take one of those." He reached into his back pocket for his wallet.

"Well . . ." Max was speechless. No one had ever offered to buy his school lunch before!

His older sister, Alex, who was also behind

the counter, nudged him from behind. "Sell it, dummy," she whispered. "You can make another one."

Alex was right. Time for some ka-ching! "That will be eighty dollars," Max announced.

"What?" the man asked in disbelief.

Even Max knew that price was crazy for just a sandwich. "Okay, four dollars," he negotiated.

The man handed Max the money, carried the sandwich over to a table, and sat down and started eating. Max couldn't believe that the man was actually eating a sandwich made up of mashed potatoes, chicken, and peanut butter for breakfast. His new creation must be a real hit! Max smiled to himself. I am an artist—a sandwich artist, he thought. Fame and fortune, here I come!

Miranda tucked a piece of her dark hair behind her ear and walked slowly around the restaurant, checking everything out carefully.

"I love your family's shop," she told Justin. "Have you ever thought of maybe blacking out the windows and painting the walls, I don't know, black?"

Justin laughed. Miranda was not like any of the other girls in their high school. She had her own unique style. "I think you are going to be easy to shop for," he joked, as they left for school together.

Harper pouted. Life wasn't fair. "He's hanging out with that Goth girl, Morticia?" she asked Alex.

"It's Miranda," Alex corrected. "Look, Harper, as your best friend, I'm going to give it to you straight. I think he really likes this girl."

Harper rolled her eyes. "Fine, but it's so totally obvious that he's dating her because she looks like me."

Alex stared at Harper in her bright blue outfit and perky red headband. She and Miranda were total opposites. Was Harper completely delusional? "Yeah, you both have . . . faces," Alex offered.

Alex wished her friend would wake up and face reality. Besides, she couldn't figure out why Harper had a crush on her nerdy older brother.

Jerry Russo, who had been straightening up the restaurant, carried a tray of empty plates and dirty napkins to the counter. "Max, you're going to be late for school." He gave his youngest son a nudge. "Get out of here."

"'Bye, Dad." Max sprinted out the door.

"Excuse me," a man called to Mr. Russo. Jerry Russo hurried over to the customer's table. The man pointed to his food. "Your son made me this sandwich."

Mr. Russo cringed. "Oh. I'm sorry. Look, he's only twelve."

"No, it's terrific." The man reached over to shake Mr. Russo's hand. "I'm Jeff Malone, concessions manager and back-up announcer for Shea Stadium. We're considering local delis to provide the official sandwich of the New York Mets."

Mr. Russo's eyebrows shot up in surprise, because Mr. Malone said the name of the baseball team exactly as the stadium announcer did—even with the echo. Amazing! he thought.

"I think you should submit this sandwich for consideration," Mr. Malone finished.

What?! Mr. Russo wasn't sure he'd heard right. "Theresa?" He reached over and pulled his wife away from another customer. "This guy"—he pointed to Mr. Malone—"is from the New York Mets, and he wants to consider *us* for their official sandwich!"

"Which sandwich?" Mrs. Russo asked.

"The one your son made," Mr. Malone replied. "'To the Max.'"

Mr. Russo sighed. Max's silly sandwich wasn't on their official menu. "Uh, that's not really—"

"A bad idea," his wife finished. "Not a bad idea at all. 'To the Max' is one of our most popular creations," she fibbed. She whispered to her confused husband, "We'll just get Max to make it for us later."

"Great." Mr. Malone stood up to leave. "My sandwich associates from the New York Mets and I will be by on Saturday for judging."

Mr. Russo grinned and did his best announcer's voice: "Great! Let's go, Mets!"

Mr. Malone had barely exited the restaurant before Mr. and Mrs. Russo began dancing and whooping in excitement.

Alex felt her cheeks turn pink. How embarrassing! "Unbelievable," she muttered, as she grabbed Harper and headed out the door to head to school.

"I know. Your parents are *so* cool!" Harper exclaimed.

Alex sighed. Her family was a lot of things, but cool wasn't the first thing that came to mind. Supernatural, sure. Wizards, yes. But nobody knew about their magical powers—not even Harper. It was a family secret. To the rest of the world, they tried to appear normal.

Alex watched her parents conga-line their way into the kitchen. She just wasn't sure this was the *right* kind of normal.

Chapter Two

Max could feel his dad impatiently standing behind him, watching closely. Mrs. Russo anxiously stood next to him. Max scanned all the ingredients piled on the counter in the restaurant's kitchen: pickles, chocolate sauce, salami, orange slices, salsa, and cream cheese. But nothing looked quite right to him.

"Come on, buddy," Mr. Russo encouraged. "Just picture the sandwich in your mind."

"Yeah, Maxy," his mom chimed in. "I've seen you make it before. What do you start off with?"

Max's palms started to sweat. He looked again at all of the ingredients before him. He had been trying for hours to recreate the "To the Max" sandwich. He had made dozens of sandwiches, but they all tasted so . . . wrong.

"I don't know," he admitted. The pressure was intense! He knew this sandwich could bring big money to his family's restaurant, if the Mets chose it. But what his parents didn't get was that he had never thought about making a sandwich before. Inspiration just came to him. Kind of like an artist creating a one-of-a-kind painting. *I'm probably some kind of sandwich-making genius*, Max thought.

Max sighed and tried to focus. "Okay, let me think. I started with licorice."

"*Licorice* on a sandwich?" His father sounded amazed.

"No," Max explained. "I ate some licorice, and then I started my sandwich."

"Oh," Mr. Russo said.

Max took a deep breath. He eyed the food in front of him and tried to concentrate. "It had ham—"

His mother grabbed a slice of ham and plopped it on the bread. "Okay."

". . . bologna, yogurt—"

"Yogurt?" cried his parents.

"That's disgusting!" his father exclaimed.

His parents looked even more grossed out than they had before. Max rolled his eyes. "That's the point." Even though his dad ran a sandwich shop, he obviously didn't get how boys his age ate. Anything that wasn't glued down was fair game. The weirder the combo, the tastier the meal.

Max stared at his half-finished sandwich. His mind was blank. The creativity had stopped flowing.

His mother started to panic. "What are we going to do, Jerry? The New York Mets want the sandwich that Max made."

Mr. Russo's eyes darted from the tuna fish to the applesauce to the radishes laid out before them. "Well, uh, maybe we can throw a bunch of stuff together like he does. Max can taste it and tell us what we are missing until we find the right combination," he suggested.

Mrs. Russo brightened. "What do you say, Max?"

Mr. Russo squatted down next to his son. In a high-pitched voice, he pretended to be Max. "Okay. Whatever it takes to help, Dad."

Max rolled his eyes. Sometimes his parents could be so immature. His father slapped him on the back. "That's the spirit, son," he said in his normal voice. He turned to his wife. "Let's go. Come on, grab a bun."

Max hoped that his parents could find the right combination of ingredients and re-create his sandwich. He had a sinking feeling that he was going to be too full to have dessert tonight.

Justin held Miranda's hand as they left the little chess club at the corner of Waverly Place and MacDougal Street. They walked together down the crowded sidewalk. He couldn't believe what a great time he was having with her. Sure, she looked a little different than other girls, but she loved to talk about books just like he did, and she played a mean game of chess.

"Weren't you scared?" Miranda asked.

"A little," Justin admitted. "Rook to queen-bishop four is always a risk, but that's just how I roll." They walked for a moment in silence. Justin couldn't focus on anything but Miranda's hand in his. Having her so close to him was suddenly making it hard to breathe. He *really* liked her. He glanced down at her hand. "Is your hand sweaty, too?"

Miranda nodded and gave a him a shy smile. "Yeah."

"I have enormous glands," Justin blurted out.

"I don't mind," Miranda said softly. She continued holding his hand.

Justin and Miranda were so busy talking that that they didn't notice Alex and Harper walking only steps behind them. "I don't get it," Harper whined. "Justin's so full of life, and she's so full of . . . Halloween."

"I don't know, Harper, maybe on Halloween she'll dress up as you," Alex teased.

Harper laughed. "She could never pull *this* off." She waved her hand up and down her cute outfit. "I make a lot of my own clothes. Oh, which reminds me, I need some more egg cartons." Harper hurried down the street to a grocer she spotted dragging trash to the curb. Harper knew design treasure when she saw it—even if it was in someone's trash.

Alex didn't even bother watching her friend run off. She was too busy checking out her brother and Miranda. It definitely looked like they were getting serious.

Justin stopped in front of the Waverly Sub Station. He looked at Miranda.

"So, I'll see you tomorrow?" Justin asked, finally letting go of her hand. He leaned in closer to her.

"Yeah," Miranda said, smiling. She stepped toward him and lifted her chin.

Justin knew this was *the* moment—the moment for their first kiss!

Suddenly he felt like he couldn't breathe. His heart pounded in his chest, and he thought he might pass out. He panicked and pulled away.

"Yeah," he mumbled. He grabbed her hand and shook it. "Tomorrow." Then he bolted into the restaurant as Miranda stood there in bewilderment.

Alex quickly followed him inside. "Shaking hands?" she cried. "Were you guys saying good-bye or closing a deal? Why didn't you kiss her?" she demanded.

Justin turned away from his sister. "It's none of your business," he snapped. He was so embarrassed. I was so close, he thought.

"Look, Justin. You know a lot of stuff about stuff people really don't care about, which is great. But I know about relationships," Alex said. "I know how girls think."

Justin whirled around. "So do I. They're right-brain dominant, and they have a slightly larger hypothalamus," he explained.

Alex rolled her eyes. "There you go again. Knowing stuff people don't care about."

Justin cringed. Alex had a point. He really didn't have a clue what he was talking about when it came to girls. "Okay, okay." He took a deep breath. It was hard to ask his younger sister for help. "I'd be open to suggestions."

"Good, because Miranda *really* wants you to kiss her," Alex told him. "I can tell. She brightens from tragic to gloomy when she's around you."

"So?" Justin didn't understand where Alex was headed with this.

"So . . . if you don't do it soon, she's going to think that you're really not into her. And then, someone's going to have to play chess by themselves," Alex explained.

"I already do that." Now Justin was annoyed. Leave it to Alex to act like such a know-it-all! "Did you ever think of this, Miss Smarty Pants? Maybe I don't *want* to kiss her!"

Alex smirked. If Justin wanted to play that game . . . "Okay," she warned, following him into the kitchen of the restaurant. "I'll be spreading *that* rumor around."

"Look." Justin knew he was going to have to be straight with Alex. "Okay, I know this is going to be hard to believe, but . . . I've never kissed a girl." He quickly looked down.

Alex laughed. "I find it hard to believe that you think that *I* find that hard to believe." Then she hesitated. She didn't want to hurt his feelings.

"All right, this is what you are going to do," she said finally. "First of all, take out five dollars."

Justin reached into his pocket and handed his sister the money. "Why?"

"I need five dollars." Alex crumpled the bill in her fist. "Second . . . tomorrow when you walk her to school, take her by that old, scary, abandoned house on the corner."

Justin brightened. "Right, because she'll think I'm brave."

"No," Alex corrected. "You'll get scared and she'll comfort you. That's when you plant one on her."

Justin smiled. His sister *was* good at this girl stuff. "Okay, that's a great idea."

"Thanks." Alex reached out her hand. "Do you have five ones for this five?"

"Uh," Justin replied, checking his wallet. He pulled five ones out of his pocket.

"Great," Alex said, as she skipped out of the kitchen. " 'Cause my five was lonely."

What a sneak! Justin was about to chase after her but then stopped. After all, Alex probably knew what she was doing. And she wouldn't even have to use any of her magic skills to make anything happen. The three siblings were all wizards in training, but they had to keep it a secret. Their parents were the only ones who knew about their magical powers. Alex was always extra careful that no one, especially the kids from school, would ever find out.

I guess I'll trust Alex and see what happens next, he thought. Maybe it's worth ten dollars to finally get my first kiss!

Chapter Three

"Does anybody see anything?" Mr. Russo asked his three kids later that afternoon. They all stared deeply into the crystal ball. The kids were attending a wizard class in their basement, or what they referred to as "the lair." Their dad gave them lessons every Tuesday and Thursday after school.

"Yeah, that little squiggly thing in the back of your throat," Max joked, pointing to his dad's reflection in the glass ball.

"Oh." Mr. Russo laughed, but he had been hoping for a different answer. He moved the crystal ball closer to the trio. "We are looking for someone at Shea Stadium making our sandwich, so we can see what's *in* our sandwich. Now, concentrate."

"If I go back in time and look into a crystal ball, will I see *me* looking into this crystal ball?" Max asked. He had just gotten his powers. He had *a lot* of questions.

Mr. Russo picked up the crystal ball and walked across the room. "Okay, that's not concentrating." He sighed in frustration. He placed the ball on a corner of a high dresser. "Now—" As he turned to face the trio, his elbow swiped the ball, and it crashed to the floor. The glass shattered into tiny pieces.

"Now *that* was cool!" Max exclaimed.

Alex stared in disbelief at all of the jagged glass scattered on the floor. Her dad looked really upset.

"It's irreplaceable. What am I going to do?" Mr. Russo cried. Suddenly he had an idea. "I know!" He pulled a large, dusty book of spells off a high shelf. He flipped through the pages until he found the one he needed. "Okay, Justin, here." He gently pulled Justin off the sofa and carefully positioned him in front of the broken glass. Alex and Max followed.

"Do this spell on the crystal ball," he instructed Justin. "When I had my powers, it was a lifesaver." His dad had given up his wizard powers when he married a mortal, their mom. But he still had the ability to teach his kids magic spells.

"Say, '*Mcreary-timereary*,'" his dad said.

"Why?" Justin asked.

"Just say it," their dad pleaded. "Oh, and do this." Mr. Russo showed Justin how to raise his arms, bring them back down, point both fingers out from his hips, and give a little wiggle as he chanted the spell.

"*'Mcreary-timereary*'!" Justin cried, doing the motions.

"Whoa!" Alex exclaimed. They were all suddenly sitting on the sofa again. The crystal ball—perfectly intact—was back on the coffee table in front of them.

"Did we just go back in time?" Max asked, excited. "I've got to learn that! *'Mcreary-time—*"

"Oh, no, no, no!" His father quickly stopped him. "That spell is just for emergencies. It rewinds time for a few seconds to give wizards a chance to correct a dire mistake."

"You mean like a do-over spell?" Alex asked.

"Yes . . . but it's too dangerous," he explained. "Don't even think about it, all right? It bends time and space, and you're not ready for it." He tried to get serious again. "No more questions."

"Do people remember if there's a do-over spell?" Justin asked.

"Only people in the magical world. Regular

87

people have déjà vu," he said. "Stop asking questions."

"So *that's* where déjà vu comes from," Justin said slowly.

"I said, no more questions!" Mr. Russo exclaimed.

"It wasn't a question," Justin replied.

"Hey, I have one," Max interrupted. "What's déjà vu?" he asked.

"Well, it's when you feel like something's happened before," Mr. Russo explained.

Alex stood up. "For example, Dad, do you have five dollars?"

Mr. Russo reached into his wallet and handed Alex a five-dollar bill. "Why?"

"'Cause I need five dollars!" Alex headed toward the door. She turned back to her brother. "Déjà vu, huh, Justin?"

She just loved how easy it was to trick her family into giving her money. And she didn't even need to use a magic wand!

Chapter Four

The next day at school, Alex pushed through the crowded halls to reach Justin at his locker. "So, how did the big first kiss go?" she asked. She waited for the juicy details.

"It didn't happen," Justin revealed sadly.

"Why not?" Alex demanded. The only thing that had gotten her through her math class was knowing her brother would soon tell her all about what had happened with Miranda.

"Because when I went to pick her up, she

didn't want to go to a scary house. She wanted to go through some dark alley instead," Justin said, disappointed.

Alex shook her head in confusion. "But a dark alley's even *better* than a scary house."

"But you said 'scary house!'" Justin exclaimed. "I was totally focused on the scary house."

How can Justin not be getting this? Alex wondered. She sighed loudly.

"The point is, she wanted you to kiss her," Alex explained. "Why didn't you take my advice? Lots of people do. I'm the one who told Vice-Principal Clements to fix his tooth. Now he's getting married."

"Okay, I panicked," Justin admitted.

"*Panicked*?" She asked him incredulously. "Well, now you got to kiss her quick, or else all she'll think you guys will ever be is just friends."

"That's never going to happen," Justin said confidently. "She's really into me, and I'm really into her."

"That could change in a hurry," Alex warned.

"No way. Everyone around here knows we're kind of going out. You know, people respect that," he told his sister.

"Oh, really?" Alex said with a smirk. How could Justin be so clueless? she thought.

"Mm-hmm—" he responded, ignoring her.

"Well, let's see about that," Alex interrupted. "Hey, Matt!" She called over a cute brown-haired football player who was walking down the hall.

"Miranda's pretty cute, right?" Alex asked him. She nodded toward Miranda, who was standing at her locker nearby, grabbing her books for class.

Matt's eyes lit up. "Yeah. You know, I got a note from her in seventh grade that said she liked me. Bet she still does, too." He stared at Miranda with interest.

"Well, that's too bad," Alex commented

sadly. "I hear she's going out with Justin."

"Who's Justin?" Matt asked.

Justin nudged Matt. "*I'm* Justin."

"So?" Matt was one of the most popular kids at school, and he knew it. Justin didn't pose any threat. He could definitely ask out Miranda if he wanted to.

Alex smiled knowingly at Justin. She was right—again. "Okay. Thanks, Matt."

"No, thank *you* for the heads up on Miranda." Matt hurried across the hall and toward the stairs. "Yo, Miranda. Wait up there a sec." He smiled at her as they walked together up the stairs.

Justin watched in amazement. "What did you just do?" he cried.

"I just proved that not only do I know girls, but I also know guys." Alex was quite proud of herself.

"No, you got Matt to ask out my girl-friend!" Justin exclaimed.

Alex looked at her brother calmly. "Oh, wait, I can fix this." She glanced around the hallway. Most kids had gone into class already. There weren't many choices. Suddenly she spotted a girl with her back toward her. She'd have to do. "Here's a cute girl. Kiss her." Alex grabbed the girl by her shoulders and whirled her around to face Justin.

Justin gasped. "This is my Spanish teacher!" Justin exclaimed, horrified. How embarrassing! "*Hola, Señora Gonzalez. Me llamo biblioteca.*"

Mrs. Gonzalez looked very confused. She gave Justin an uneasy smile and hurried away.

Justin groaned. "I think I just told her my name is 'Library.'"

"Well, Mr. Library," Alex teased. "You should check out a book on kissing."

"Thanks a lot." Justin said in embarassment as the final bell for class rang. He sighed loudly. What was he going to do now?

* * *

Later that afternoon, Justin refused to talk to Alex as they walked home from school together. He silently stormed up the stairs to their apartment. He tossed his backpack to the floor and headed to the kitchen to grab something to drink. He wanted to feel sorry for himself in peace.

But Alex was never going to let that happen. She tossed her bookbag onto the shag rug and stood in front of Justin. "Look, Justin. I'm really sorry, but you have to admit, Mrs. Gonzalez is a young-looking teacher."

"You know what, I don't care about Mrs. Gonzalez. I care about how my girlfriend's going to the movies with a guy that my sister set her up with!" Justin exploded. It turned out that Alex *had* been right after all. The gossip in school that afternoon was that Matt had asked Miranda out on a date. He slammed the refrigerator door shut.

Alex sighed. Her brother could be so dramatic! "Will you relax? It'll all work out, because I know relationships."

"You keep saying you know things, and you don't," Justin argued.

"Hey, I was right about Miranda wanting to kiss you," Alex pointed out, "*and* I was right about Matt thinking she was pretty."

"Okay, fine, you were right. Feel better? 'Cause I don't." Justin plopped onto one of the bright orange sofas in the living room.

Alex sat beside him. "Look, Justin. The only thing getting in the way here is *you*."

"You know what, I know," Justin admitted. "I've had a ton of chances to kiss Miranda, and I'm just mad at you because I am mad at me."

Alex wrinkled her nose in confusion. "You *are*?" Justin is taking the blame for *me*? Now this is something weird, she thought. Weird—but good. "Yeah," she quickly agreed. "You are."

"And if Miranda is ready to kiss me, you

know what?" Justin asked. "I should be ready to kiss her. And it's not too late."

"Yeah. It's not too late," Alex agreed.

"And this time, I'm going to be ready," Justin vowed. He stood up and danced in place. Then he wrapped his arms around an imaginary girl and gave the air a huge smack with his lips.

"What are you doing?" Alex asked.

"Starting my training!" Justin announced. *Boxers train for a fight, runners train for a marathon, so I am going to train for the most important moment in my life—my first kiss! Justin thought.*

He had a plan. For the next couple of days, he would focus on nothing but kissing. He would totally be in the kissing zone.

That evening, in the empty Waverly Sub Station kitchen, Justin opened the refrigerator and found exactly what he needed. He reached in and lifted out a molded ring of red Jell-O.

He shook it and watched it jiggle. It looks just like a girl's lips, he thought. Justin leaned over, closed his eyes, and gave the cold Jell-O a big kiss. When he opened his eyes, he saw his father in the doorway watching in complete confusion. Yikes! There's no good way to explain this, Justin thought.

The next day, Justin had a better idea. He grabbed Max's soccer ball from the floor of the bedroom. Then he borrowed a tube of lipstick from his mother's dresser. RED HOT, the label read. Justin smiled. After I'm done practicing, my kisses will be red hot, he thought. He drew a pair of red lips on the ball with the lipstick.

He ran downstairs, sat on the sofa, and gazed at the soccer ball. He moved the ball closer to his face. He closed his eyes—and kissed the lips of the ball. Suddenly the soccer ball was yanked away.

Justin's eyes flew open. Max made a gagging

gesture, grabbed his soccer ball, and headed out the door to practice.

"Oh, my!" his mother gasped, as she walked into the room. She stared in horror at her eldest son with bright red lipstick smeared all over his mouth. Justin grimaced. What could he possibly say?

That evening, Justin mopped the restaurant floor after closing. He pretended he was at a new club downtown. The music was pumping. He and Miranda were grooving. He twirled the mop to the beat in his head. He flipped the dirty mop around, so the wet fabric now looked like long hair. A girl's hair. A girl who wanted to be kissed by him. Justin leaned the mop back, reached over, and planted a kiss on its imaginary damp lips.

"Gross!" Alex cried, horrified, from behind the counter.

Justin glanced at the dirty mop he had just kissed. Training was over. He was ready.

Chapter Five

Max sat at the end of one of the booths in his family's restaurant. Sandwiches were piled high on the table in front of him. He took a bite out of a huge sandwich and chewed thoughtfully. He swallowed and shook his head. "It's close, but this one has too much teriyaki."

"Honey, we didn't put any teriyaki on it," his mother gently reminded him.

"Then it needs teriyaki," Max decided.

His dad put his head in his hands in frustration. Then he pointed wildly to all the sandwiches on the table. "This one has too much cheese, this one needs barbeque sauce, and this one tastes like armpit. How do you even *know* that?"

Max shrugged his shoulders. "Wrestling," he explained.

Mrs. Russo touched her husband's hand. "Honey, calm down. Max is doing the best he can."

"Right. I know." Mr. Russo exhaled loudly. He took a deep breath and put his arm around Max. "Buddy, I know you are trying as hard as you can. It's just, if we can become the official sandwich of the New York Mets, our lives will be gravy!"

Max gasped. "That's what's missing!" he cried. "Gravy!"

"Gravy!" his mother exclaimed. "Then

what are we doing standing around talking about it?" She grabbed the sandwich in front of Max and brought it over to the counter. She used a ladle to pour gravy on the sandwich. She quickly put the sandwich back together and presented it to Max.

"Oh, come on, gravy. Come on, gravy. Come on," his dad chanted.

Max took a bite and swallowed. He leaped up from the table and yelled, "That's it! 'To the Max!'" He pumped his arm in victory.

"Whoo!" the three of them cheered.

"'To the Max!'" Mrs. Russo exclaimed.

Max's sandwich was definitely a winner.

Meanwhile, across town, Miranda sat next to Matt in a darkened movie theater. The movie hadn't even started yet, but she couldn't think of anything to say to him. The date was kind of boring. She chipped away at her black nail polish.

"So, uh, I heard you're going out with a guy named Justin," Matt said awkwardly. "Right?"

"I thought we were, but I don't know," Miranda admitted.

"That's cool," Matt replied.

What's cool? Miranda wondered. She had the feeling that Matt's brain was the size of a Tic Tac.

"Yeah, totally," Matt continued. "Do you play video games at all?"

Miranda turned to stare at him. "Do you know who makes video games?" she demanded.

"No," Matt admitted.

"Corporate America," Miranda replied. "I *hate* corporate America. I'm starting a school club about it. We're looking for sponsors."

"Hey, guys!" a male voice suddenly rang out.

Miranda and Matt stared in surpirse at Justin, who was standing in the aisle beside them. Matt gave Justin a polite nod.

Miranda instantly perked up. She nudged

Matt. "Hey, Matt. Why don't you go get us some popcorn?"

Justin smiled. "Yeah, I'll buy." He pulled some money from his pocket and handed it to Matt. "Here." He was willing to pay anything to get this guy far away from Miranda.

Matt stared in amazement at the bill in his hand. "Twenty bucks? Thanks, dude. I can go play some Nitro Burning Funny Cars. Oh, yeah!" Matt stood up and ran up the aisle and toward the lobby.

Justin slid into Matt's empty seat and leaned toward Miranda. "Why are you here with him?" He tried to disguise the hurt in his voice. "We're kind of going out."

"I know we hold hands and stuff, but you act like we're just friends," Miranda said defensively.

Justin sighed. "She was right," he muttered under his breath.

"Who was right?" Miranda asked.

Alex popped up from behind their seats. "Me. I was *so* right. I'm the one who told him that if he didn't kiss you soon, you were going to think that he wasn't all that into you. And that's what you were thinking, right?" She rested her arms on their seat backs, sticking her head between theirs.

"Alex, what are you doing here?" Justin demanded.

"Look, I felt bad," Alex said. "So I came down here to make sure you kiss her."

"You were going to kiss me?" Miranda asked Justin with a smile.

She's smiling, Justin realized. She likes the idea!

"Well, it's not a surprise now, is it?" Justin said, giving his sister his best get-out-of-here-now look.

"Sorry," Alex apologized. "I'll be back here if you need me." She pointed to the rear of the theater. She squeezed her way down the row.

"Shhh!" several moviegoers warned Alex.

"All right, just for that I'm leaving my cell phone on," Alex taunted. She slid into a seat in the last row of the dark theater and leaned forward. She still had a perfect view of Justin and Miranda. They were staring intently at each other.

Alex smiled and nudged the girl next to her. "Oh, look at those lovebirds. It's so great when things work out." She turned to the girl and reeled backward. "Harper? What are you doing here?"

"I'm not Harper," Harper whispered. "I'm just a theater seat, keeping an eye on my boyfriend."

Alex did a double take. Harper was wearing a dress and a hat made out of the same dark gray woven fabric that was on the seats! "You made an outfit to match the theater seats?" Alex asked her best friend incredulously. Harper's crazy creativity always amazed her.

Harper pulled her hat over her eyes. "Don't be freaked out if you can't see me." At that moment, she caught sight of Justin cozying up to Miranda. "It's time to go to work." Safely disguised, Harper began to sneak down the rows.

Alex laughed. Her friend actually *did* blend in with the seats. Justin would never see her coming! She turned her attention back to Justin and Miranda.

"You were going to kiss me?" Miranda was asking Justin again.

"Well, only if you wanted to kiss me. Do you?" Justin asked nervously. "Or is me asking totally ruining the moment?"

"Nope." Miranda smiled. She inched closer.

Alex crossed her fingers. She watched Justin slide toward Miranda. Here it comes, she thought.

Suddenly, Justin and Miranda bumped noses. *Hard*.

"Oh!" Miranda cried, pulling back.

"Ah," Justin groaned. This was not supposed to happen! But, then again, the soccer ball and the Jell-O didn't have noses. He had forgotten to factor in that obstacle.

"I'll go left. You go right," he suggested.

Miranda looked confused. "Then we'll both be going the same way."

"Oh, yeah." Justin realized that wouldn't really work, since they were facing one another. "Uh . . . let's both go left." He leaned closer to her.

Miranda leaned away from him. She bit her lip. "Justin, I'm a little nervous," she admitted. "This is our first kiss."

Justin acted cool—like he'd kissed many girls before. "Don't worry. I'll guide you through it." Her nervousness suddenly gave him confidence.

He was ready to kiss her. He lunged toward her—and knocked over the supersized soda in the cup holder in front of her. The icy liquid splashed all over Miranda's lap. She cried out in surprise.

"Miranda, I'm so sorry!" Justin wanted to crawl into a hole. Could he be any more clumsy? He stood up and hurried into the aisle. "I'll get some napkins."

Alex raced into the aisle, too. "Where are you going?" she demanded in a whisper. "Why didn't you kiss her yet?"

"I spilled soda all over her," he hissed. "She's never going to kiss me now."

"Wait!" Alex grabbed his arm. She'd had the BEST idea! "Do it over."

"What do you mean?" Justin whispered.

"The spell Dad used on the crystal ball," she said excitedly.

"No way," Justin said. "Dad said that was for emergency use only."

At that very moment, cold soda and cubes of ice rushed down his back. He whirled around in shock. What had just happened? he thought.

Harper, looking oddly like a theater seat, was standing beside him, an empty cup in her hand. Justin stared at her in bewilderment.

"Just because you don't know I'm your girl-friend, doesn't mean you can sneak around behind my back!" Harper snapped. She stormed out of the theater.

Justin looked over at Alex in confusion. Now what was he supposed to do?

"How does that do-over spell sound now?" Alex whispered.

"Like it should have happened already," Justin said through clenched teeth.

Alex smiled. "Now we're talkin'." She raised her arms and brought them down to her hips and wiggled her body as she chanted, "*'Mcreary-timereary'*." Bright lights flashed from her hands, and then . . .

Suddenly, Justin and Miranda were brought back in time!

"Justin, I'm a little nervous," Miranda

admitted, exactly as she had said it before. "This is our first kiss."

"I know." Justin looked around. "I mean—" Justin quickly took the big soda out of the cup holder and placed it on the floor. "—let me move this."

He leaned toward Miranda and closed his eyes. He started to kiss Miranda when . . .

"Ahhhmmm," someone growled by his face.

Justin's eyes popped open—and he almost hurled. He wasn't kissing Miranda. He was kissing the big belly of a man walking down the row behind them. Gross!

"This is going to be a long night," Alex said to herself, as she watched her brother from the aisle. There was only one way to fix this. She lifted her arms again.

" '*Mcreary-timereary*'!" She hoped the spell would work this time.

Chapter Six

Meanwhile, back at the Waverly Sub Station, Mrs. Russo smiled as she placed two large sandwiches in front of two men wearing fancy suits. One was Mr. Malone, and the other was named Mr. Kaminsky. Mr. Kaminsky also worked for the New York Mets. He'd told them what his specific job was earlier, but she had been way too nervous to pay attention. Please, oh, please like the sandwich! she silently begged.

Both men raised their eyebrows when they saw the size of the sandwiches.

"And that's why it's called . . ." Mrs. Russo began.

" 'To the Max,' " Max, Mr. Russo, and Mrs. Russo chimed in.

The three of them stood anxiously around the table. They watched as both men took big bites.

"Nothing like it in the city," Mr. Russo remarked.

"Kind of a buffet on a bun," Max added. Do they like it? he wondered. It was hard to tell.

"What did I tell you?" Mr. Malone told his partner. "Is this the sandwich for the New York Mets or what?" Max held his breath as Mr. Malone made the team's name echo. What would the other guy say? he wondered.

"You're right," Mr. Kaminsky agreed. "This is delicious."

Max wanted to perform a victory dance right there, but he controlled himself.

"Congratulations, Mr. and Mrs. Russo," Mr. Malone said. "'To the Max' is now the official sandwich of the New York—"

"And that's why it's called . . ." his mother suddenly said.

"'To the Max,'" Max, his mother, and father said in unison.

Whoa! We're back at the beginning again! Max realized.

He turned quickly to his dad. "Dad, what just happened?" he whispered.

"I don't know," his father said, bewildered.

The two men each took a first bite of their sandwiches.

"Good . . . but kind of familiar," Mr. Malone remarked.

"You're right," Mr. Kaminsky agreed. "It's tasty, but familiar."

"Familiar?" Mrs. Russo asked in confusion.

Max's brain was spinning. What was going on? he thought.

"And that's why it's called . . ." his mother suddenly said again.

" 'To the Max,' " Max, his mother, and father chimed in once more.

Max was so confused he didn't know what to say. Everything was happening all over again, as if it had never happened before!

Once again, the two men took first bites of their fresh sandwiches. Once again, they chewed while Max and his parents watched nervously.

Mr. Malone shook his head in disappointment. "Nothing really new here."

"You're right," Mr. Kaminsky said. He pushed the sandwich away from him. "A better name would be déjà vu, because somehow I feel like I've tasted this before."

Mr. Russo pulled Max aside. "It's the do-over spell," he whispered to his son.

Max raised his arms. "I swear I'm not doing it."

"I know," his dad said with a sigh. "But I'm pretty sure I know who *is*."

Max knew that his brother and sister were in a whole cauldron of trouble now!

Back in the movie theater, Justin and Miranda tried to kiss again. But Justin let out a huge burp instead!

Miranda pulled back in shock. Justin's face burned in embarrassment.

Alex sighed. Is Justin *ever* going to get this right? she wondered. She was starting to think not.

"*'Mcreary-timereary*'!" she called out again. Sparks flew from her hand, rewinding time. Justin had yet another chance.

Miranda moved toward Justin. Justin leaned toward Miranda. They closed their eyes. Their lips were just about to touch when, suddenly,

Justin let out another noise. Only this time it didn't come from his mouth!

Miranda looked disgusted.

"Gross!" cried Alex. She waved her brother over. "Justin, that's seventeen do-overs already," she hissed. "What's wrong?"

"I'm nervous," he admitted. "I'll get it this time." He hurried back to his seat.

"Okay, fine." Alex lifted her arms over her head. "*'Mcreary-ti—*"

Just then, she saw her dad hurrying down the aisle toward her. Yikes! Alex quickly dropped her arms to her sides. "Hi, Daddy!" She gave a little giggle, trying to look innocent. "So, how'd the sandwich tasting go?"

"I don't know," her dad said in annoyance. "It's still going on . . . and on and on." He gave his daughter an 'I-know-what-you've-been-up-to' look. She knew she was busted.

Justin quickly walked over to his father and sister. "Dad, what are you doing here?"

"No, the question is what is Alex doing the do-over spell for?" Mr. Russo demanded. "I specifically told you never to use it."

"Actually, it's my fault, Dad," Justin whispered. He stood in front of his dad, trying to block him from Miranda's view. "I'm here with Miranda, and I'm—"

"He's trying to have his first kiss," Alex interrupted, "and he just can't get it right."

"First kiss?" Mr. Russo sounded amazed. "I thought that happened years ago."

How humiliating! Justin thought.

"I'll just take Miranda home," Justin said, disappointed.

"Wait, Justin." His dad turned toward Alex. "How many times did you use that spell?" he asked her.

"I don't know. Seventeen?" she guessed.

Mr. Russo thought for a moment. "Well, I guess if you break a rule seventeen times, an eighteenth doesn't make a difference." He put his hand on his son's shoulder. "Justin, do you think you could get it right, if we do it over one more time?"

Justin smiled gratefully. "Yeah," he replied.

"Okay," Mr. Russo said. "Alex, do your magic."

"Thanks, Dad," Justin said. Then he scooted back to his seat and leaned toward Miranda.

"'*Mcreary-timereary*'!" Alex chanted. Sparks flew from her fingers, and her brother had one final chance. He better not blow it this time, Alex thought.

Chapter Seven

After the movie ended, Alex and Justin hurried back to the Waverly Sub Station with their dad. They were anxious to find out if Max's sandwich was a hit.

Mr. Russo looked around the empty restaurant. Mr. Malone and Mr. Kaminksy were gone. Max and his mom were silently cleaning the tables. Neither of them looked happy.

"So, I guess we're not the official sandwich of the New York Mets, huh?" he asked.

"The last thing they said was that after one bite, they were tired of eating it," Max reported.

"Isn't that weird?" Mrs. Russo asked.

"Yeah. Weird," Alex agreed. She felt bad that she had messed up their big chance at inventing a famous sandwich.

Mr. Russo brightened and pulled his wife aside. "Justin got his first kiss!" He grinned. "Don't make a big deal."

"Your first kiss!' Mrs. Russo squealed. She dropped the cleaning rag and hurried over to her son. "Oh, my baby, you are growing up!"

"Mom!" Justin cried. So much for his mom not making a big deal about it! Justin turned to Alex, who was now sitting by herself at a table. "Hey, how about you, Alex? What was your first kiss like?'

Alex twirled the ketchup bottle nervously. "Oh, you know," she said nonchalantly. "Like everyone else's."

"You already had you first kiss, and I missed

it?" their mom cried. "Oh! Tell me, tell me everything." She stood over Alex, ready for the details.

Mr. Russo's eyebrows shot up. "No, not *everything*. She's my little girl." He turned to Alex. "What's his name? I'll make him cry," he promised, doing his best tough-guy impression.

"Jerry," Mrs. Russo scolded her husband. She knew no one was really going to be scared by him—he was such a teddy bear!

"Tell us about it, honey," Mrs. Russo encouraged Alex.

Alex looked at the ceiling and then looked down at the floor. She wasn't sure what to say. "Um, i-it was at this place . . . with this guy. And, um, it was very romantic. Over Christmas vacation," she stammered.

"We went to see Grandma and Grandpa over Christmas," Max piped up.

"Hold on," Justin said, "she's lying." He

walked over to Alex. This was going to be soooo good! he thought. "You haven't kissed anyone! I totally have this over you," he declared.

"No, you don't!" Alex argued. She tried to sound like she didn't care.

"You're right," Justin said smugly. "So when I go to school tomorrow and tell everyone you haven't kissed anyone, no one will care."

Alex grimaced. She could *not* let Justin do that. If everyone at school knew, well, she didn't think there was enough magic in her dad's spell books to fix the damage to her reputation.

She had no choice. She would have to work some magic of her own . . . and quickly!

The next day at school, Justin stood against his locker and gave Miranda a kiss. Then he spotted his sister coming down the hall.

He kissed Miranda again, making sure Alex got a good look. Ha! How superior am I? he thought.

"Hey, Justin," Alex called. Her eyes darted around, checking out all the kids at their lockers. She didn't have a lot of time to be choosy.

A-ha! She suddenly spotted Matt, Miranda's date from the night before. She grabbed him by his shirt and pulled him over to her. Without a word, she planted a huge kiss on his surprised lips.

She released Matt and whirled around and faced Justin. "Now you've got nothing over me!" she announced.

Alex headed to her next class . . . with a stunned Matt trailing behind her like a lovesick puppy and her brother staring at her in awe. She smiled. Victory was hers, once again!

Something magical is on the way!
Look for the next book in Disney's
Wizards of Waverly Place series.

Spellbound

Adapted by Beth Beechwood

Based on the series created by Todd J. Greenwald

Part One is based on the episode, "Alex's Choice," Written by Matt Goldman

Part Two is based on the episode, "New Employee," Written by Peter Murrieta

Best friends Alex and Harper get invited to rude 'n' rotten Gigi's annual tea party, and to Alex's horror, Harper is psyched to go. But when Alex learns Gigi's plan is to humiliate Harper, she decides to use her magical powers to teach Gigi a lesson she'll never forget!

Plus, when Alex uses a spell to help Harper with her job at the Waverly Sub Station, the magical mishaps are endless!